Donated by...

LAFAYETTE SUBURBAN
JUNIOR WOMEN'S CLUB

COYOTE AND THE ~~WITHDRAWN~~

A Pacific Northwest Indian Tale

COYOTE AND THE FIRE STICK

A Pacific Northwest Indian Tale

Retold by BARBARA DIAMOND GOLDIN

Illustrated by WILL HILLENBRAND

GULLIVER BOOKS

HARCOURT BRACE & COMPANY

San Diego   New York   London

Thanks to Chris Johnsen and
Kristin Skotheim Barber for their help
—B. D. G.

Requests for permission to make copies of any part of the work should
be mailed to: Permissions Department, Harcourt Brace & Company,
6277 Sea Harbor Drive, Orlando, Florida 32887-6777.

Gulliver Books is a registered trademark of Harcourt Brace & Company.

Library of Congress Cataloging-in-Publication Data
Goldin, Barbara Diamond
Coyote and the fire stick: a Pacific Northwest Indian tale/retold by
Barbara Diamond Goldin; illustrated by Will Hillenbrand. — 1st ed.
p.   cm.
"Gulliver Books."
ISBN 0-15-200438-6
1. Indians of North America—Northwest, Pacific—Folklore.
2. Legends—Northwest, Pacific. I. Hillenbrand, Will, ill. II. Title.
E78.N77G65   1996
398.2'0899'0795—dc20   94-5747

Printed in Singapore
First edition
F E D C B A

The illustrations in this book were done in oil and oil pastel on paper.
The display and text type were set in Xavier Sans Medium.
Color separations were made by Bright Arts, Ltd., Singapore.
Printed and bound by Tien Wah Press, Singapore
This book was printed with soya-based inks on Leykam recycled paper,
which contains more than 20 percent postconsumer waste and has a
total recycled content of at least 50 percent.
Production supervision by Warren Wallerstein and Ginger Boyer
Designed by Kaelin Chappell and Will Hillenbrand

With love to my brother Bert and his family—Nancy, Aaron, and Rosie   —B. D. G.

To Ricky   —W. H.

IN THE TIME BEFORE THE PEOPLE HAD FIRE, they ate their fish and meat raw, and in the winter their lodges were cold and dark. They knew about Fire. They could see it burning on top of a high, snowcapped mountain. But they dared not try to take it, for they knew that three evil spirits guarded Fire.

One very cold and snowy day, wily and crafty Coyote passed through the People's village. The People drew all about him.

"Coyote, you have taught us so many things: how to make fish traps and how to spear salmon, how to dry the fish and store it for the winter," they said. "Now we need Fire. We are tired of the cold and the dark. You are so wise, Coyote. Can you help us get Fire? We cannot do it without your help."

The People's words flowed all around Coyote, tickling the hair about his ears and spreading a grin about his shining white teeth. The words flowed into his mouth, down into his chest, puffing it out so. He liked the feeling.

"I'll think of a plan," he answered them.

As Coyote left the village, he still heard the People's words of praise trailing behind him. He swam across the river and ran through the meadow to the forest at the base of the very high mountain. The words helped him climb all the way to the top.

As he climbed, Coyote could hear the mumbling and giggles of his sisters. They could take on many shapes and today had chosen to be round purple huckleberries nestled in his stomach. It was an easy way for them to travel—let Brother Coyote do all the work.

"See how your chest puffs out so," said one sister in her tiny huckleberry voice.

"You think too highly of yourself," said the other.

"*Sssh,*" said Coyote. "You will have to be quiet if I am to get Fire from these evil ones. Do you want to do your own walking?" The huckleberry sisters didn't. They quieted down and Coyote found a place to hide behind a large boulder near the lodge of the evil spirits.

Coyote hid and watched for hours. It was cold there, but he would not give up. Not Coyote. He watched all the while an old and gnarled evil spirit guarded Fire.

And he watched all the while the second spirit, with its long stringy black hair that hung down across its face, guarded Fire.

When the second one went inside the lodge, Coyote was still there, hiding and watching. But the third one did not come out right away. It was dawn and very chilly, and this one was slower about coming out to watch Fire.

Aha, thought Coyote, *dawn is the time to steal Fire.*

Coyote began to dance his way down the mountain,
oh so happy with himself. Until he realized one thing.
He knew when to steal Fire, but he didn't know how.
That was another matter.

So Coyote stopped his dancing and started his thinking. He thought very hard. But as hard as he thought, and as wise as he was, not one idea came to him. He decided to ask his sisters.

Coyote thumped on his stomach and called, "Sisters! The People want Fire from the mountain. Tell me a plan for the People."

"We do not want to tell you," answered one sister in her tiny huckleberry voice. "You will say that you thought of the plan all by yourself, just as you always do. The People will think you are so wise and your chest will puff out even more."

"Hmph," said Coyote. "Then you will have to do your own walking."

"Oh, all right," squeaked the sisters. "We will tell you a plan."

When they finished, Coyote grinned. "Why, that's the very same plan I thought of myself."

"That brother of ours!" his sisters complained. "We can't trust him!"

But Coyote paid no attention to them. With their plan simmering in his head, he ran down the mountain to the forest, gathering the animals as he went. He called Mountain Lion from the rocky ledges of the mountain, Deer and Squirrel from the forest, and Frog from the river. When they were gathered together, he told each one what they were to do and where they were to wait. Each one's place was in a line between the People's lodges and Fire.

Coyote went back up the mountain. As he climbed, he could hear the tiny rumbling sounds coming from his stomach. His huckleberry sisters were still complaining.

"*Sssh!*" he warned severely, and they stopped.

Coyote reached the lodge and hid. He watched the first evil spirit. Then the second. When the second one went inside the lodge, Coyote was still there, hiding and watching. Now was his chance.

Coyote jumped out from his hiding place. Quickly, for Coyote was quick, he grabbed one of the sticks whose end burned with Fire. He clutched the cool end with his teeth and ran with the stick down the mountain.

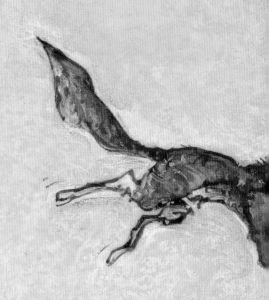

But the evil spirits were also quick. From the door of their lodge, the third evil spirit saw Coyote steal Fire and called to the other two. All three of them chased after Coyote.

He could hear their angry, grunty noises behind him. And as the evil spirits ran, their big bare feet showered Coyote with ice and snow from above. *Hold on*, Coyote encouraged himself as he ran. *You will see Mountain Lion soon.*

Coyote could feel the evil spirits' hot breath on the fur of his back. He smelled it too. Then one of them grabbed the tip of his tail.

"*Yow!*" howled Coyote through gritted teeth. He almost dropped the fire stick. But he kept on, and there was the rocky ledge where Mountain Lion waited.

Coyote tossed the fire stick to Mountain Lion, who caught the
cool end of it with his strong teeth.

"Run fast," Coyote warned.

And Mountain Lion did. He leapt from one rocky ledge to another,
down the mountain, until he came to the forest where Deer waited.

Mountain Lion tossed the still-burning stick to Deer, who carried it through the forest. The evil spirits were not far behind. They jumped over the brush and sticks and in and out of the trees following Deer, growling and grunting as they ran. They were not as graceful as Deer, but they were almost as fast.

At the forest's edge, Deer saw Squirrel waiting. Deer tossed the fire stick to Squirrel. Squirrel caught the cool end of it with her teeth. But Squirrel was so small and the fire stick was so big that it bumped against her neck as she ran and burned a black spot there. The fire stick was so hot it made her straight tail curl up.

But Squirrel could not linger to look at her neck or her tail. Oh no. Not with these three evil spirits after her. Squirrel skittered across the meadow.

Squirrel saw Frog waiting near the river and tossed the fire stick to him. By now the fire stick was small and hot. Frog couldn't wait to reach the other side of the river, the side near the People's village.

Frog hopped and hopped. Just as he reached the riverbank, the third and youngest evil spirit caught up to poor Frog. It grabbed Frog's tail in its claws and would not let go. This hurt Frog so, but it did not stop him. He jumped into the river anyway and left his tail behind.

The water felt good. Frog swam and swam. The evil spirit swam too, splashing and shouting. It caught up to Frog on the other side of the river.

Frog was frightened. He looked this way and that. He could not give up Fire. Then he saw a tree close by. Frog spit what was left of the fire stick onto the tree. The tree swallowed Fire.

The other two evil spirits caught up with the third one. They all grumbled and argued, poked and pulled. But they could not get Fire out of wood. They did not know how.

Still grumbling, the evil spirits stomped back to their lodge on top of the mountain. They were certain that the People would not be able to get Fire out of the tree either. But clever Coyote knew how. He showed the People the way.

Coyote rubbed together two dry sticks of wood from the tree that had swallowed Fire until sparks came. He used these sparks to make wood chips and pine needles burn. He made a great fire from these chips and needles for the People. They used Fire to warm their lodges and cook their meat and fish.

"Coyote, thank you for your plan," said the People.

"Coyote, you teach us so many things," they said.

"Coyote, you are always welcome here."

The People's words of praise followed Coyote out of the village, making him strut and prance as he walked. He felt good all over—except for the grumbling and rumbling noises coming from his stomach. But really, this did not bother wily and crafty Coyote very much.